FAl

~ ᴅᴜᴄ

Written by Ava Armstrong

Dark Horse Romance
Novella Series

CHAPTER 10

~ Ella ~

The moment Ella's eyes opened, the smell of stale popcorn and uneaten food assaulted her. Her first reaction was to pull the blanket over her head. But she immediately thought of Ray and making out with him in the front seat of the car the night before. As she smiled to herself, Cassie and Paige were up and pulling the blanket off her. Where they got their energy, she'd never know. She had ignored them last night, but knew that tactic wouldn't work for long. This morning her friends were all questions, asking what happened.

As the blanket was finally yanked off her, Ella screamed, "It was only dinner!"

Ella did not like waking up in chaos. However, Cassie and Paige were relentless. They were hitting her with a pillow and they continued asking questions about Ray.

"It was only dinner and we talked ~ that's all." Ella repeated for the umpteenth time.

Finally, the girls took turns using the shower and sharing the hair dryer. After an hour of primping, they were ready for breakfast. Ella had sent a text to Ray, *meet us at the diner with the big neon light that says breakfast just down the street.*

As the girls piled into the Honda they flattened their canvas bags to make room for the items they would purchase on their day-long shopping spree. Although Ella couldn't even *think* about shopping; all she had on her mind was seeing Ray again and how sweet his kiss was last night. How sweet *everything* was with him. She had only left him eight hours ago, but she missed him already.

Cassie's voice brought Ella out of her daydream, "I am starving."

Paige added, "Yeah. I'm hungry, too."

Cassie touched Ella's shoulder, "I noticed the way Ray looked at you when you signed those legal documents last night, Ella. He's interested. I have noticed you have drifted away from Bob lately ~ or, more accurately, he's drifted away from you."

Ella didn't want to delve into the fine details of her dysfunctional relationship with Bob in the car but she acknowledged Cassie's observation, "Yes, there have been long absences lately. Bob is different somehow. I don't know. The spark is gone. Not to mention he hates my dog. I never realized I was sleep-walking through life until I met Ray. There's a sweet quality about him; he has warmth, kindness."

Cassie commiserated, "I've been dating Steve now for what…six months? I don't even *know* where the relationship is going. I don't even think *he knows*. He just has so much going on. It's hard having a relationship with a guy who's in a band. He travels constantly, just like Bob does. It gets lonely sometimes. You know what I mean, Ella. You and I end up on the phone most nights, watching television or going to a movie or dinner."

Paige lamented, "Well, at least you both *have* a boyfriend. I'm a free agent right now. The last two I dated were *complete losers*. If I wanted a teenage boy, I'd adopt one. At least the guys you're with have jobs. I liked Ray. He seemed like a responsible serious type of guy. And, I think he's kind of cute in a Neanderthal sort of way."

As they pulled into the diner, Ray's Cadillac was already there and Ella felt her heartbeat quicken.

"Hey, isn't that Ray's car right there." Cassie pointed out the obvious.

"Yes, I might have mentioned we were coming here for breakfast." Ella lowered her eyes and tried to feign innocence. But she noticed the raised eyebrow Cassie and Paige exchanged as they entered the diner.

Ray immediately greeted the girls and they were seated in a booth. "So, how did you ladies sleep last night?" Ray asked them, Ella thought he sounded polite. And, he looked ruggedly handsome with his hair slicked back. He hadn't shaved and the scruff made him look even more masculine, if that was possible.

"Is that *you* that smells so good?" Cassie said to Ray, and Ella felt a wave of embarrassment sweep over her.

"I took a shower this morning," Ray smiled, "And, I put on some stuff that supposedly drives women wild. Bottega Veneta, it's Italian, like me."

Paige giggled. Cassie yammered on about last night's shopping spree minus Ella. Paige was flirting shamelessly with Ray, hard to ignore, as she was seated right next to him. Ella observed every detail from the opposite side of the table. Paige might have pulled a muscle in her neck turning to look at him as she did. Finally, Paige sat sideways in the seat so she could talk with Ray directly. Ella felt the sting of jealously creep over her. She had never felt this way when Bob was showered with compliments from other women. With Bob, Ella only felt disappointment and occasional depression as a result of his constant criticism, but never jealousy.

But as Paige attempted to capture Ray's complete attention, Ella felt his foot tap hers beneath the table a couple of times to get her to look into his eyes. His deep set, dark blue eyes glanced her way and Ella couldn't resist. Just making eye contact made her feel giddy. After the food arrived, the girls settled down and ate. This gave Ella a chance to talk with Ray quietly. Ella didn't want to expose her true feelings for Ray, not just yet. But she knew in her heart she was falling in love with him.

"How was your evening last night?" Ella managed to ask Ray with a courteous tone.

When his eyes locked with hers he said one word, "Heavenly."

Ella noticed Ray had that cute little smirk on his face and knew he was referring to the action in the front seat of the Cadillac. Cassie and Paige were talking but no one was listening. For a split second, it was as if Ray and Ella were there alone together just gazing at one another over a stack of hot blueberry pancakes.

"I hope you have a safe drive home." Ella said politely, meanwhile noting the warm smell of blueberries intermingled with his cologne. She couldn't pronounce the name of it but the scent succeeded in driving her wild. She wanted to talk to Ray privately but it wasn't possible with the two girls there. Every so often, the girls would laugh loudly or co-opt Ray's attention briefly interrupting their exchange. Ray insisted on paying for breakfast and Cassie and Paige smiled and thanked him.

As they piled into the Honda, Ray touched Ella's hand before getting into the car. "Wait." He whispered.

"Thank you." Ella said as she gazed into his face. She wanted more than anything to kiss him goodbye, but the parking lot was crowded and noisy. The smell of fresh rain and motor oil lingered, but Ray looked and smelled wonderful. As she let go of his hand, she watched him walk to the Cadillac and get in. The car represented Ray, old-fashioned, unique, sturdy and enduring. She wasn't sure, but she thought she detected a little spring in his step. He smiled and waved, then drove away.

Ella stood near the open door of her Honda for a moment as she watched the tail lights of the Cadillac get swallowed up in the traffic. He was gone. And for a split-second Ella wondered if she would ever see him again. Then realized it would have to be soon because she couldn't bear the thought of *not* seeing him. It was as if her very life depended upon it. Cassie and Paige were yelling for her to get in, and she did.

"Hey, Ella, he's a sweetheart ~ I'll take him." Paige whispered.

Cassie was filled with renewed energy, "That was nice of him to pay for breakfast….but I think he did it because of Ella, not us."

Ella remained silent as she drove to the outlet strip malls. There were miles to go before they'd sleep and she didn't want to waste energy chattering about Ray with them. She loved her friends but they could be annoying sometimes. Right now she just wanted to remember the touch of Ray's hand upon hers and the intensity in his dark blue eyes. If she didn't know better, she thought he might have been on the verge of tears. And, oddly enough she felt the same way.

The shopping trip began with housewares and toys, but always ended up with clothing and jewelry. Once gifts were selected for those on their Christmas lists, the girls always indulged themselves giving gifts to one another. It was a pre-Christmas celebration that turned out to be more fun than Christmas itself. As Ella giggled, tried on clothing, and pretended to walk the catwalk in the dressing room, her thoughts were not on shopping. She couldn't think of anything but getting home and planning the next time she would see Ray. She wondered how long it would take him to drive back to the city. She hoped the traffic wasn't horrible.

She wondered what Ray's apartment was like. Was he happy there? She wanted to go to see his apartment when he scheduled the meeting with Marina. But she also thought about what might happen if the two of them were together for an entire weekend again. Alone. Together.

Replaying the time at the fishing camp, she wished she could have been as daring as Cassie and Paige. They would have ripped off his clothes and caressed him from head to toe. But Ella held back knowing it wouldn't have been the lady-like thing to do, especially when she already had a boyfriend. But she was caring less and less about Bob's opinion of her. She was tired of being told what to wear and how to act, living under a microscope of scrutiny and, worst of all: suffering through his passive-aggressive commentary. His attitude of superiority was a huge turn-off. She didn't deserve any of that. The mere thought of Bob always served as a wet blanket that extinguished any flame of excitement she had lately about anything. She could no longer envision a future with him.

After shopping with the girls, Ella filled up at the gas station for the drive home. Cassie and Paige resurrected the subject of Ray.

"I thought he had a great personality." Cassie expounded.

"I thought he had a great ass." Paige blurted out. "Well, he *did!*"

"What about you, Ella? What do you like best about him? Cassie asked.

Ella drove in silence for a moment, then responded, "He's gracious."

Cassie laughed, "Gracious? You mean polite and a gentleman?"

Ella gave her a sidelong glance, "Yes, exactly."

"So, what did you talk about at dinner last night?" Cassie asked.

"We had a serious conversation." Ella said. "It was deep."

"About what?" Cassie was digging for more details.

"Ray is going to set up a meeting between me and my father's mistress." Ella exhaled after saying the words. They were not easy to utter.

"No kidding." Cassie was genuinely surprised. "Why would you even *want* to meet *her?* She broke up your parent's marriage, didn't she?"

"Yes," Ella replied, "But, my father broke up the marriage, also. It takes two people to make that happen. I've always been curious about Marina. It's hard to explain. She loved my father very much. And, I know that he loved her. I've just always wondered what she was like. I want to meet her, that's all."

"I don't think I could do it." Cassie murmured.

"I'd want to punch her in the face," Paige muttered.

"I don't feel that way," Ella continued. "I want to just get to know her a little bit."

"So, you will go to New York City to meet her?" Cassie asked.

"Yes, next week. Ray will set it up." Ella answered.

"Where will you stay in the city? Will you stay with Ray?" Cassie queried.

"Of course not, silly. I'll get a hotel room." Ella smiled.

"I'd love to go to New York City," Paige volunteered.

"Yeah, how about it, Ella? All three of us could go together?" Cassie offered.

"I think I want to do this alone." Ella replied somberly.

Eating breakfast across from Ella in the diner was a treat for Ray and it reminded him of the first time he met her. He only knew Ella for a short time, but driving home it seemed like he had known her forever. Meanwhile, as he started the long journey back to his empty life, he felt he might die until he got to see her again. And, that became his focus, setting up the meeting with John Wakefield's mistress. Driving back to New York City, Ray phoned Marina and told her about Ella's request.

He had been prepared to spend some time trying to convince John Wakefield's mistress to meet Ella, but surprisingly, Marina was more than happy to do so. In fact, she said she had always wanted to meet John's daughter but figured it would not be possible because of the situation. She was not proud to be the woman in the shadows, as she put it. Marina seemed to fear nothing. She was a public figure all of her life, dealing with lunatic fans and crowds of worshippers wishing they were her.

As Ray pulled the Bluetooth off his ear, he thought about Ella shopping with her friends. She was so unlike them. Cassie and Paige seemed immature, almost as if they were stuck in their teens. Ella, on the other hand, was different, worldly and intellectual, wise beyond her years, with a touch of youthful innocence. There was something about the look she gave him over the pancakes this morning. What emotion was reflected in her green eyes? He felt it was love, plain and simple. She was thinking the same things he was, reading his mind ~ he just knew it.

He plugged the Bluetooth back in while sitting in a long line of traffic and tapped the speed dial for Ella. He had to hear her voice. She picked up immediately and he heard her answer sweetly in his ear. Ray inhaled and said, "Hi, I just wanted to hear your voice. I'm not interrupting, am I?"

There was a momentary pause and she replied, "Hi Ray, is everything all right?"

"I just want you to know I've set up a tentative meeting with Marina for next Saturday. I'll contact you with the date and time, but she's excited and happy to meet with you. Who wouldn't be?" Ray mused.

He heard Ella's breath on the phone, "Thank you. I don't even know *why* I want to meet Marina. It's almost as if knowing her will make me understand some things that happened, sort of fill in the blanks, you know? Thanks for setting that up so quickly."

"I can't wait for you to come to New York City. I can't wait to be with you again. You understand that, don't you?" Ray whispered into the speaker while driving. "I'm maneuvering through traffic and I can't stop thinking of you. I'm sorry, I shouldn't have interrupted your shopping trip."

"No, it's fine. I needed a little break. Cassie and Paige are trying on clothes." Ella laughed. He loved to hear her laugh. But it only made him miss her more.

"I'll send you a message on Facebook tonight." Ray said. "Or, would you prefer that I call you?"

He listened while Ella hesitated for a moment. "Send me a message on Facebook. I'm not sure what time I'll get home exactly."

"I will." Ray's heartbeat quickened. He disconnected the call. The rest of the long ride home was spent listening to music. It seemed every song reminded him of Ella. He never realized how many love songs there were until now. When he was with Sarah, which seemed like a hundred years ago, he never thought about songs or anticipated seeing her ~ not like this. But, he was a different guy then. Being wrapped up in hockey and his college friends made his relationship with Sarah different. She was the girlfriend. He made love to her, but could barely remember what it was like. He knew one thing for sure, he never felt the intensity when he kissed Sarah that he did with Ella. Not even close.

He wondered when Ella would move out of Bob's country club house on the golf course. The sooner, the better, in his opinion. But she hadn't mentioned a step-by-step plan to move out. She was returning to live there after the shopping trip. And, Ray would be contacting her on Facebook. Nothing had really changed except he wanted her more than ever. And, she was coming to New York City next weekend, although she didn't commit to that just yet.

He imagined all of the places he would take her. He wanted to kiss Ella on the top of the Statue of Liberty and on top of the Empire State Building. *Damn, he just wanted to kiss Ella.* There was this one little Italian place, very expensive but worth every dime. While in traffic he called and made the reservation. He knew the owner, a friend of Tony's. He secured the perfect corner table and explained it was a special occasion. It would cost him hundreds but that didn't matter. He wanted everything to be perfect when Ella was with him.

He also wanted her to bring Boomer with her. She could drive down and he would meet her at the park 'n ride just over the bridge. She could follow him into the city without confusing directions. He remembered one of his coworkers mentioned leaving town next weekend. He'd find out if Ella could leave her car in his space in the firm's parking garage.

Like a love-sick teenager, he began counting the days before he'd see her again. Tomorrow was Sunday. He was planning to take a ride to see Pops to tell him about seeing Ella again and to thank him for the Cadillac. If only he knew how much he enjoyed taking Ella to dinner in it and kissing her in the front seat. Pops would get a kick out of that.

He had thought about almost everything except his apartment. It was a bachelor's pad for sure ~ code for a mess. He contacted his good friend, Rosa, from Tony's, on his way home.

"Hey, listen, I have a girl coming next weekend. What can you do with my apartment to make it look like a human being lives there?"

Rosa had a wonderful laugh. She ran a cleaning and staging business and worked one or two nights a week at Tony's only because she liked him and was distantly related. "Oh, not to worry. I can work wonders in a week. How much money do you have?"

In bed that night he tossed and turned, once waking and immediately his thoughts went to Ella. Kissing her in the front seat of the car was heavenly, all right. And, the long hot shower afterward helped to relieve his frustration for a little while. But he had a burning desire to undress her, make her feel like a woman who was loved and appreciated. He suspected that hadn't occurred in a long time, if ever. Ella never mentioned any guys in her life prior to Bob. He wondered if Bob was her first.

He hated even thinking of Bob being with Ella, having her all to himself. He didn't deserve her. Ray knew he was making a snap judgment from afar, but somehow sensed he was right on the money. Something about this Bob character just didn't add up. Although Ray had never met him, from Ella's description, Bob seemed aloof, uncaring, self-centered and downright annoying. Ella deserved someone who would love her and care for her, like a real man. Not some self-centered metro-sexual jerk who spent more time in the mirror that she did.

For the remainder of the night he tossed and turned in bed. His thoughts finally quieted and he slept from sheer exhaustion. The last cognitive thought he had was Ella spending the night in his apartment with him, just the two of them, kissing, undressing in his bedroom. A pleasant thought, indeed.

~ Bob ~

Even though it was a Sunday, Bob scanned his computer to find the phone numbers for Blake Ricker and Stan Collins. They were the two owners of the law firm Ray Adriano worked for. Blake would most likely be home watching football, something extremely distasteful to Bob, but nonetheless that was the man's passion. Blake had once dreamt of playing for the NFL but had long-term injuries from high school that prevented him from living that dream. Bob remembered meeting Blake for the first time. They were introduced by John Wakefield on the golf course at The Club.

He listened to the phone ring, once, twice, and the third time it went to voicemail. He knew he had to leave a message, "Hey, Blake. It's me, Bob Albertson. I have something to talk with you about and it's urgent. Call me." He hung up.

He didn't even think of apologizing for calling on a Sunday afternoon. This was important. He needed to know everything about Ray Adriano as soon as possible. He wanted to greet Ella at the door tonight when she arrived and confront her about the iPad and her Facebook conversations. But, before that would happen, he wanted to have Ray Adriano officially removed as her attorney.

Thirty minutes passed and Bob found himself pacing back and forth in front of the television. He knew this was the football game Blake was watching because Blake timed his return call for half-time.

"Hey, haven't heard from you in a while. How can I help you?" Blake sounded curious.

"I have something to talk with you about, it's urgent." Bob huffed.

"I'm all ears. What can I do for you?" Blake said.

"There's an attorney working for you who is representing my fiancé, and I want him removed from her case." Bob demanded. "The guy's name is Ray Adriano."

"Whoa, wait a minute, buddy." Blake said deliberately. "First of all, congratulations on the engagement. Ella Wakefield, is it? You've been with her now for what, two years?"

Bob wanted to cut through the small talk, "Yes, we got engaged a few days ago."

"And, what about Ray Adriano? He's one of my best guys. We're promoting him this coming week from associate to attorney. Why do you want him removed from Ella's case, if I may ask?" Blake asked with a somber tone.

"He's been messaging Ella on Facebook. He's chasing her skirt, if you must know." Bob blurted, feeling his blood pressure rise.

"So, what's the big deal about that? Any nude photos? Foul language? What exactly was the conversation?" Blake sounded unconvinced.

Bob grabbed the iPad and opened it. He read each message to Blake on the phone, feeling like an idiot. He described the photos of Ella and Ray with the puppy at the train station. Finally, after what seemed like twenty minutes, Bob stopped talking.

"Sounds to me like they are Facebook friends." Blake responded. "Has Ella made any complaint about Ray?"

"What the hell are you talking about? This guy is chasing the woman I want to be my wife, for God's sake! Can't you see how he is sweet-talking her?" Bob felt his face flush, his hand trembled.

Blake laughed ~ *actually laughed* ~ and this caused Bob's anger to intensify. How could he take this so lightly? "I want this guy off the case, Blake. Their relationship has crossed the line from attorney-client to something deeper." Bob insisted.

"Not happening." Blake said nonchalantly. "Ray Adriano is a professional through and through. And, I'm not taking him off Ella's case without *Ella* asking me to do so. I'm sorry you feel this way, Bob. But, I am telling you this guy is one of my rising stars. I think you need to be talking to Ella, not trying to interfere with Ray Adriano's career path."

Bob hung up the phone in a state of disbelief. *His rising star?* That's how he saw this goofball associate attorney? It was painfully apparent that he couldn't get Ella assigned to a different attorney. The next step would be to order a complete background check on Ray Adriano. He sat in his recliner and popped up the screen to order the background check. Within minutes he had the details of Ray Adriano's whole life on his laptop. He went over every detail and could find nothing out of the ordinary. Adriano never so much as had a parking ticket. Figured. This guy was probably a Boy Scout.

The only weak area he found was financial. Adriano owed money for college loans, had a paltry savings account and a 401k that was just beginning to produce. Hitting him hard financially would be the next step. There was one guy he knew who might be able to help, but it was a long shot. He worked for the Internal Revenue Service. Bob played golf with him. Maybe, just maybe, he could get his friend to go over a copy of Ray Adriano's tax return line by line and find a *reason* to have him audited. That would be painful. But, it wasn't enough. *He had to find another avenue to teach this punk a lesson and to drive him away from Ella for good.*

The phone rang and it was Ella. "Hi Bob, I'll be home soon." Her voice sounded cheery. No doubt she had dinner with Ray Adriano Friday night and it was probably romantic. He felt his blood pressure rise and tried to control his rage.

"Bob, are you there?" Ella asked.

"Yes, honey. Can't wait to see you. What time will you be here?" he managed to ask with a courteous tone.

"I'm dropping off Cassie and Paige right now. Did you want me to pick up something for dinner?" Ella offered.

"Sure." Bob couldn't think straight. "Whatever you want, honey."

"Okay, I will stop on the way home. Anything special that you'd like?" Ella seemed so damned happy. Her voice was somehow different.

"Whatever. I'm not all that hungry." Bob said flatly.

He paced the floor in silence as he waited for her car to pull into the driveway.

CHAPTER 11

~ Ella ~

Bob sounded strange when she spoke with him on the phone. Maybe she had awakened him from a nap or interrupted a business call. She knew how he hated that. He didn't sound too cheery, but that was typical. Ella dropped off Cassie and Paige and stopped at Bob's favorite Thai place on the way home.

As she drove into the driveway, she left everything in the car and ran next door to Molly's to retrieve Boomer. Molly answered the door and the puppy came straight through. Ella fell to her knees and Boomer licked her face.

"Oh God, I've missed you so much!" Ella squealed. She scooped the puppy up and brought him outside. Ella watched as Boomer hopped around excitedly in the grass. Every time she looked at Boomer, she thought about Ray. She wouldn't have him if it hadn't been for Ray. She had a pang of loneliness for a moment. She'd miss Ray very much until next weekend.

She walked back inside with Boomer and paid Molly for dog sitting.

"I love him." Molly exclaimed. "You can leave him with me whenever you like."

As Ella approached the door of Bob's house, it was already open and he was standing in the doorway. "The dog is more important than I am. I see where I stand." Bob said, his words dripped with sarcasm.

"I had to get him, Bob. He's been waiting for me. He's only a puppy." Ella explained, but her words didn't matter. Bob seemed to be in a bad mood, worse than usual. Ella put Boomer inside and hauled the shopping bags into the mud room and closed the door. She grabbed the Thai food from the front seat and walked into the kitchen hoping Bob would be in a better mood after eating.

Bob was sitting at the table with her iPad and Ella swallowed hard. She had forgotten she left it there and wondered if she had been forgetful enough to leave her Facebook account automatically-logged in. When Bob's blue eyes met hers, she instantly knew he had read the exchanges with Ray.

"Hungry? I'll put this stuff in a dish," Ella pretended she didn't notice the iPad.

"No. Sit down, Ella." Bob commanded her. "We need to have a little talk."

Ella noticed the vein pulsing on the side of his head and knew his blood pressure was definitely up. The look on his perfectly tanned face was one of simmering rage.

Ella sat at the table and Bob opened the iPad and went through every photo, every message, and finally asked in an accusatory tone, "What's this all about, Ella?" His face flushed with anger and his eyes seemed to bore through her.

"We are friends, he is my attorney." She daringly reached over to close the iPad. "Besides, this is *my* iPad and Ray is *my* attorney. *This is none of your business.*"

Enraged, Bob stood and paced back and forth in the kitchen, "None of my business? Really? You are my fiancé and this is none of my business? You have lived here with me for almost two years and this is none of my business? I am trying to *protect* you, Ella. Don't you see this guy is coming on to you? This is highly irregular behavior for any attorney." Bob ranted. "It's unprofessional. Put an end to this, Ella. I mean it. If you don't, I will." Bob left the iPad on the table and stormed out of the room.

Ella picked Boomer up and buried her face into his fur. The puppy had been cowering beneath the table. Holding back tears, she fed the hungry pup. Then she sat at the table alone as she picked at the Thai food. Apparently, Bob wasn't speaking to her now. She could hear him upstairs in the master bedroom and knew she couldn't sleep there with him tonight. He was in a state of anger she had never witnessed before. For a moment while he was yelling in her face, she actually felt oddly afraid of him. She hated feeling vulnerable and she hated Bob for making her feel this way.

For a long while she stayed in the kitchen with Boomer. She knew the best way to end it was now. But where would she go? She took Boomer for a short walk and called Cassie. Thank goodness she picked up on the first ring.

"Ella, did you get home all right?" Cassie asked sleepily.

"Yes. But I have a big problem and need your help. Can you come over here tonight while I pack my stuff into my vehicle? I need to sleep on your couch tonight. I've had a terrible argument with Bob, I'll explain it later. But, I'm leaving."

Ella exhaled a sigh of relief when Cassie agreed to come right away. When she stepped back into the house, Ella could hear Bob on the phone and the television was on in the master bedroom. She really didn't want to have another confrontation with him. She started collecting everything that was hers from the first floor of the house, which wasn't much.

She looked at her phone with the thought of sending a text to Ray. She was pleasantly surprised to see that Ray had already sent her one, *I miss you so much, I feel like I can't breathe until I see you again. I'm sorry, Ella, I'm in love with you.*

Ella messaged him back: *Bob found the iPad and read our messages. He is angry. Cassie is coming over. I will stay at her place tonight. I am afraid of Bob. His face turned red and he was yelling at me. I miss you, too.*

Ray instantly responded: *You've got to get out of there. Do you need help?*

Ella wrote back: *I will stay with Cassie tonight. I have an idea. I have a real estate client. They have a beach house for sale, and they've already moved to California. It's really cute. I've thought of buying it. Could you help me with that?*

Ray answered: *Of course. Give me the contact information for the owner. I will call them and buy it for you, if you want it. Will cut a check from the trust. But need to move quickly. I want to help you.*

Ella wrote back: *Yes, that would be perfect. I need to be alone with Boomer. It's over with Bob. I think it was over a while ago, but I just couldn't seem to face it.*

Ray replied: *I can't wait to have you here with me this coming weekend. I love you, baby.*

Ella wrote back: *I've got to go.*

She stumbled into the kitchen searching for the cord to charge her phone. As she did, Bob was standing there. She didn't hear him come down the stairs.

"What are you doing down here?" Bob asked angrily. "Aren't you coming upstairs to bed?"

"No," Ella said firmly. "I think it would be better if I slept at Cassie's tonight. It's over, Bob. We are not getting married. I don't want to live here any longer."

She immediately wished she hadn't made the comment. It only served to reignite the whole conversation. Bob's face became red and he paced around her in an odd sort of way, as if he didn't know how to handle the feeling of relinquishing control. When he glanced at her, Ella sensed he was immersed in dark thoughts.

Strangely enough, Bob begged her, "Come upstairs, Ella, please. You think finding that stuff on Facebook made me happy? Am I supposed to just ignore what's going on between you and this associate attorney? But, the anger quickly returned as he puffed up and bellowed, "I called his superiors today. I'm having him removed as your attorney. The guy is a creep!"

Ella stared at him, "This is *not* about my attorney! It's about you and me, Bob. We are finished. We want different things in life. It's nobody's fault. That's just the way it is." She looked away. The sight of his red, contorted face reviled her. She suddenly wondered what she ever saw in this guy. The horrible thought flitted through her mind: *I've just wasted two years of my life with this jerk.*

"You're not leaving, Ella." Bob moved closer searching her face with his eyes. "I won't let you leave here tonight."

Ella felt anger simmering inside, "Don't waste your time. I'm not staying, Bob."

He stepped closer to her and suddenly she heard Cassie's car in the driveway. Ella ran to the door and opened it. A confused Cassie stood on the threshold out of breath, "Is everything all right?"

Ella instantly pulled Cassie inside, "Please help me pack my stuff."

Bob stared transfixed at Cassie as if he could punch her. But Cassie exuded defiance with her body language and stood in front of Ella shielding her from Bob. Once he knew he couldn't get his way, he backed off. Cassie marched up the stairs to the master bedroom following Ella, and a feeling of relief followed. It was times like this that Ella appreciated Cassie's determination and spirit. She was a spitfire.

Like a petulant child, Bob stood in the doorway silently. But the expression on his face said everything. He was enraged, red-faced, and frustrated. Ella asked him to move so she could carry armloads of clothing down the stairs. Silently, his rugged form disappeared around the corner. She exhaled. She didn't like confrontations with Bob. He was much bigger and stronger than her and was known to fly off the handle in anger on a regular basis. But tonight was the worst.

As Cassie brought the last box downstairs, Ella scooped up Boomer and brought him to her car. Bob was nowhere to be seen. She thought she heard him in the upstairs master bedroom before she closed the ornate front door of his house for the last time. She was glad he didn't try to stop her. She would have just forged ahead. In her heart, she knew it was the right thing to do. Oddly, she didn't feel a twinge of sadness; she only felt relieved that she was escaping the jaws of something terrible that defied description.

As she followed Cassie to her nearby apartment, Ella let out a sigh of exasperation. "Don't unpack this stuff." Ella said when they parked in Cassie's driveway, "I'll get on the phone tonight. I'm calling California, there's a three-hour time difference. It's only 9:00 PM out there right now. I think I can be in a place by tomorrow."

Ella noticed the look of disbelief in Cassie's eyes, "Really? You're calling California? Who? Ella, you've got to tell me what the hell is going on!"

Ella hugged her, "I will, right after this phone call. Now please be a good friend and run a hot bath for me?"

Cassie ran a hot bath in her cast iron tub while Ella cuddled with Boomer searching her phone for the number she wanted. Ella placed the call to the Andersons, the family who had already moved who still owned the beach house. She caught Mrs. Anderson on the second ring.

"Hi, it's Ella Wakefield. I have a few questions for you." Ella said.

"Oh, hello, Ella. Do you have a buyer for the house?" Mrs. Anderson asked.

"Yes. I want to buy it." Ella said with confidence. "I'll have my attorney send you the money, $400,000 right?"

"That's wonderful, Ella! Such a pleasant surprise!" Mrs. Anderson exclaimed. "We are so glad you will be the one living there. It's a beautiful place. We miss it so much."

"You don't love California?" she asked.

"Oh gosh, Ella. It's very different from Maine. We miss the East coast." Mrs. Anderson sounded sad. "But, I suppose we will adjust."

Ella smiled. "Thank you. My attorney will arrange a quick closing on the property. I'm sure I will be happy there. I have one more huge favor to ask of you."

Mrs. Anderson said, "Sure, ask anything."

"Can I move in tomorrow and lease it while the closing is in play?" Ella asked, crossing her fingers.

"Certainly. Is there something wrong, dear? I mean, you sound like you're in such a hurry." Mrs. Anderson asked politely.

"Actually, I just broke up with my live-in boyfriend and needed to get out of his house as soon as possible ~ like tonight." Ella stated somberly. "It's a long story."

"I understand, dear." Mrs. Anderson's voice was filled with concern. "Call me if you need anything else. And, Ella – if your boyfriend bothers you, call the police. Be careful, dear."

Ella hung up the phone wondering if Bob would bother her. She had no way to predict his behavior. It took her one hour to pack her car and Cassie's to the roof with everything she owned. There was a book collection she left behind. Hopefully, if Bob was congenial enough, she'd get it back someday. But, right now she had all that she needed.

Cassie yelled to her, "Hey, Ella, the water is almost to the top." Ella ran to the bathroom and Cassie perched on the vanity chair. "Okay, Ella, I want the full story, now." Cassie proceeded to give herself a facial as Ella explained everything in great detail.

Ella's clothing slipped to the floor and she immersed herself into the hot water. Boomer curled up on her pile of clothing. The dog's eyes seemed to be filled with relief mirroring Ella's mood. Rehashing the angry argument with Bob, Ella filled Cassie in on every little detail. The Facebook conversations, talking with Ray, the friendship they had formed, and most importantly, how her relationship with Bob had unraveled over the course of time.

Cassie responded, "Jeez, Ella, I thought you were going to *marry* Bob. I never knew the relationship was so….awful."

For a long moment as Ella soaked in the hot bath, she looked at Cassie, "I never knew the relationship was so awful either, until I met Ray. At first I just liked Ray as a friend. He was so sympathetic. He listened to me talk about my dad. He is a caring person. He has this genuine kindness about him. Bob never mentioned my father's death. Even when I cried he didn't hold me. Come to think of it, he wasn't even there when I was crying. He was away on another business trip."

Cassie listened, and being the good friend she was, she immediately gave Ella her undivided attention with a healthy dose of sympathy. As Ella finished speaking, Cassie stood and walked out of the bathroom with the green facial mask drying on her face. "I'll get you some blankets and a pillow for the couch, Ella. And, I will make you a cup of hot chocolate, I think you need that."

Thinking of Ray while alone in the tub, Ella began wishing she was already living in the bungalow and it was the weekend. She was looking forward to the visit to New York City. As she got out of the long soak, she watched the water swirl around the drain in the tub and for a moment she felt as if all of her tension slipped away with it. She toweled off and peered at herself in the mirror. She was exhausted and thought she could see worry lines around her eyes. "I'm too darned young for this." Ella murmured to herself. Cassie had kindly retrieved Ella's bathrobe from the car and left it on the vanity chair.

Cassie's couch was lumpy but Ella was so exhausted she fell asleep within minutes. In the morning, Ella dressed, took Boomer and drove to the office to get the keys to the bungalow. One of the brokers in the office covered her phone and morning appointment for a showing.

It took Ella two hours to unload everything at the beach bungalow. The salty brine of the air hit her the moment she stepped out of her vehicle and she inhaled deeply. She loved the smell of seaweed and saltwater. There was nothing like it. Boomer ran around the small fenced yard, it seemed tailor-made for him. Cassie stopped by the beach house at lunchtime and unloaded the remainder of Ella's belongings. "Pizza party here tomorrow! Paige can't wait to come over." Cassie waved as she drove away.

Ella busied herself hanging up clothing in the closets and filling the shelves with food from the grocery run. She found mismatched dishware in the cabinets that was ancient but charming. As her eyes took in the place, she decided she wouldn't change a thing. Even the neutral beach colors were perfect. The furnishings were brand new with comfortable slip-covers.

As soon as Boomer's dog bed was on the floor, Ella watched him crawl into it and he started chewing on one of his new toys. Ella grabbed her phone and tapped Ray's number. His deep voice boomed over the speaker, "Ella?"

"I'm all moved in, Ray." Ella exhaled. She was excited and relieved all at the same time.

"Oh, damn, I've got to come and see you. Can I?" Ray whispered.

"Yes." Ella replied. "I'd love for you to come, Ray."

"I'll take a couple of days off and drive up. I'm leaving right now." Ray whispered. "See you in a few hours."

~ Ray ~

As Ray stopped by Blake Ricker's office to let him know he had to make a property purchase for Ella Wakefield in Maine, Blake pulled him inside and closed the office door.

"Ray, I just want you to know that Bob Albertson called me. He wanted me to remove you as his fiancé's attorney." Blake informed him. "I refused and said Ella would need to make that request. I just wanted to let you know, this guy is bad news. You've got to watch your step with him. He's powerful, loaded with money, and doesn't like to lose, if you get my drift."

For a moment, Ray was stunned. "First of all, Ella never said she was his fiancé. Secondly, I'm glad you told me he called you. I didn't think he'd stoop that low."

Blake's brow furrowed, "Be careful, Ray. That's all I'm saying. If this guy is pissed off you're with his fiancé, there's no limit to what he will do."

"Are you sure he said fiancé?" Ray uttered. "Ella never said she was engaged to him."

"Well, he said she was his fiancé on the phone. Just watch your back. This guy's a shark in every sense of the word. I don't trust him." Blake reiterated.

"Hey, before you go, there's one more thing." Blake reached out his hand to shake Ray's, "We're promoting you from associate to attorney; that means your name will be on the letterhead. It's official. Congratulations."

Ray was pleasantly surprised and shook Blake's hand warmly. Blake was a big man, once a football player, and Ray always felt a sense of camaraderie with him. They'd both been sidelined from their favorite sports and they shared a level of integrity in business dealings that was unspoken but renown in the legal community.

"Thanks, I'm grateful for the confidence." Ray murmured.

"You've earned it." Blake chortled. "Now go save your damsel, but beware of the dragon."

As Ray opened the door to leave, Blake added one more thing, "And, don't forget, if you end up in the sack with Ella Wakefield, that's conflict of interest. You'll have to hand off her business matters to another attorney here at the firm. Just a reminder."

Ray nodded, "I know that, Blake, and will abide by the ethos of my profession. Wouldn't have it any other way."

~ Bob ~

This wasn't the way events were supposed to unfold for Bob Albertson and he was incensed. When he woke the next morning his head was pounding. He had too much to drink last night, but the throbbing in his head was nothing compared to the knife he felt in his heart.

Ella was his. *He owned her.* He knew she was trying to leave him, but couldn't accept it. *He wouldn't accept it.* Period. She was a lovely young woman, soon to be his wife, and he didn't want any other guy getting close to her, ever. He couldn't remember the last time he begged a woman like this ~ actually he had *never* made such a fool of himself. Usually women begged *him.*

Ella might try to leave him, but he would follow her to the end of the earth. He realized that he had to get her to trust him once again. And, that was his goal – Ella's complete trust. *And, the trust her father had left her.* He knew she stayed with Cassie last night, so he'd start with her. Cassie worked at a bank in the middle of town and he knew she took her lunch break at 1:00 PM.

He sensed this was only a temporary setback in their relationship. It was common for women to get cold feet just before consenting to marriage. He wanted to have the wedding at The Club as soon as possible. He would even offer to make all of the arrangements and pay for everything. Also, he wanted Ella to give up her real estate job. It sapped her energy and she had no reason to work now that she was incredibly wealthy. She could travel with him.

It would only be a matter of time before Ella would see things *his* way. She could sell her father's properties in Maine and live off the money for the rest of her life. *In fact, rolling her money into his portfolio was his ultimate goal.* John Wakefield had been a very good friend, indeed. A golfing buddy, a fishing pal, but most of all he connected Bob with his beautiful daughter who came with a massive endowment. The only way to honor John Wakefield would be to take care of Ella and her financial legacy forever. That was his noble intention.

As Bob pulled the Mercedes into the bank parking lot, he noticed Cassie's vehicle was just pulling out and it was packed to the top with Ella's personal belongings. He followed her as she wound her way through traffic and turned left onto the road that took her eastward to the beach. After a fifteen minute drive, he saw Cassie turn into the driveway of an ugly little beach bungalow. Rather than stop, Bob drove up the street and parked.

He watched as Cassie backed her vehicle up to the house and Ella emerged. The two women unloaded the car and a short time later Cassie drove away. So, Ella somehow got access to a beach rental, and, in record time. He wondered how she did this so quickly or if she had it planned all along. But then he realized she had hundreds of real estate connections.

Wanting more than ever to go inside and talk with Ella, he realized it might not be the wise thing to do. Not just yet. He drove around the neighborhood and then by her house one more time. He couldn't imagine she'd want to move from his million-dollar country club home into this squalid little place, but no matter. She'd be back as soon as he could get rid of the attorney swooning over her. His attention turned to Ray Adriano. He had a plan for him and decided to put it into action sooner rather than later. He didn't want their relationship to develop any further than it already had.

~ Ray ~

Blake Ricker seemed ominous when he spoke about Bob Albertson, almost as if he knew more about him than he wished to reveal. Ray knew Blake had a history with the guy and wondered if there were things about Bob Albertson he wanted to warn him about, but couldn't do so because of attorney-client privilege. It was just a thought that ran through his mind.

Ray was a surprised when Blake told him he would have his name on the letterhead of the law firm. The promotion came sooner than he anticipated. His income would increase dramatically and he would be taking on more cases.

But Blake's warnings about Bob stayed fresh in his mind, tempering his happiness with the promotion. One other point Blake mentioned was also foremost in his mind: conflict of interest. Blake encouraged him to go help Ella Wakefield. But he also told him if he ended up in love with her, he'd have to cease being her attorney. And, Ray knew it was the ethical thing to do.

Deep down, he knew he had already begun to cross the line into a personal relationship with Ella, thus he knew he wouldn't be able to represent her legally. But, he would put everything into the hands of a co-worker who was reliable and trustworthy. He would look out for Ella's best interest one desk away, staying involved.

Ella. He couldn't wait to see her. He felt like a teenager and hurried to get to the Cadillac to beat the traffic out of the city. But first he had to run up to his apartment. He tossed some clothing into a bag, along with his razor and shaving cream. Then threw the good cologne in, with the hope it would be his lucky charm.

The drive to Maine was five hours straight with one brief stop. When Ella gave him the beach address he put it into his phone and listened to the GPS give him robotic directions. When he arrived in Maine it was nightfall and the early evening rain pelted against the windshield of the car. The beach community she lived in was enveloped in darkness. There wasn't even light from the moon or a streetlamp. He drove slowly through the maze of roads close to the beach and came upon Ella's new residence. It sat on the road that ran parallel to the waterfront, on the sandy beach of Rough Point.

The front porch light was on and the place was charming, just as she had described it. He parked the Cadillac behind her Honda filling up what was left of the tiny driveway.

As he opened the door of the car, the rain soaked him. He'd left his jacket in the backseat. He didn't care about the rain. He stepped upon the porch and when Ella opened the door to the cottage his heart beat quickened. The moment his eyes met hers, he knew he had made the right decision. He opened the screen door separating them and swept Ella into his arms.

His lips brushed against her hair and his backpack slid to the floor. He cupped her face in his hands and whispered, "You have no idea how much I have wanted to do this." His mouth touched her lips and an instant heatwave traveled through him. As he kissed Ella, he felt her fingers touch the back of his head and she gently drew him closer.

He kicked the door closed and wrapped his arms around her feminine form. Exploring her curves with his hands fueled his longing. Every hormone in his body came alive. Even though he'd just driven five hours straight, he felt a surge of energy that he knew would be sustained for hours.

Sexy and soft, Ella's lips were eager and her breathing erratic. He had no idea where the bedroom was. But he didn't care. He'd make love to her on the floor. He could think of nothing else.

His mouth dropped to her neck and she let out a sigh that encouraged him further. Knowing the beauty that existed beneath the buttons on her shirt, he quickly unfastened them as she continued running her fingers through his hair, urging him to continue. She coaxed his lips to hers and he hungrily complied. She allowed his tongue to explore the velvet warmth of her lips until they parted, allowing him in. French-kissing Ella was incredibly sensual. Her whole being seemed to be filled with waiting and wanting him.

In a frenzy, his lips seared a path down her neck, to her shoulders. Ella's hands grasped his and she pulled him to the sofa. As she stood next to him he couldn't stop gazing into her half-closed eyes. He knew she wanted him. He had dreamt of this moment ever since he first met her. He couldn't stop the hard pulse of his arousal as it strained against his jeans. As his lips devoured Ella's, he guided her hand and she instinctively unbuttoned his pants and he felt them slide to the floor.

Rational thought left his mind at that moment. He focused on Ella's silky skin. He felt her hands exploring him and the sheer pleasure of her touch nearly drove him over the edge. It was as if he couldn't speak, he was spellbound in a trance of passion. He wanted her so much, but didn't want to move too quickly. This wasn't just sex for him. It was a deep and meaningful expression of love. He wanted nothing for himself, only to please her. He let her take the lead, not knowing how much experience she had, or lacked. He only cared that her experience with him was sensual perfection wrapped in undying love.

The dim lamplight illuminated her pink nipples and carnal pleasure drove him to tease her with his tongue. Ella let out a wild cry of excitement. He felt the ragged breath escaping her lips and he moved his mouth to her abdomen, tracing a path slowly as she writhed with anticipation. Her wiggling only heightened his arousal to another level. She arched her back and thrust her breasts upward.

Ray gazed at her and realized she was entranced with pleasure; she never looked so beautiful. With her face blushing, Ella's long dark hair tousled around her. She was panting. His exhilaration increased as he watched her coming closer to the brink.

~ Ella ~

Ray's lips touched her like a whisper. A shot of heat went through Ella as he unbuttoned her shirt. He gazed into her eyes as he slipped her shirt off. Then his eyes dropped to her pert ivory breasts in the soft lamplight. The seduction was complete as he seemed to take in every detail. His masculine hand swept over her firm breasts tenderly caressing the pink buds. As Ray's mouth suckled her nipple, she felt him gently tugging her pants off. Her hands instinctively ran through his hair pulling him to her breast. His tongue expertly circled her nipple and she was immersed in the delicious sensation. She closed her eyes and arched her back with pleasure as she felt his hardness against her thigh.

His mouth skillfully placed slow kisses along her neck making her shiver. He caressed the tip of her nose, her eyes, and finally her soft willing mouth, nearly driving her crazy with desire. She drank in the sweetness of his kiss. She loved the feeling of his hands as he skimmed the soft lines of her waist, her hips, her thighs. Clutching his hair with her fingers, she inhaled sharply as his mouth traced a path along her abdomen. His hand gently parted her thighs and Ella was breathing erratically, gasping with anticipation as his finger found the soft wet spot between her legs. Ray's touch was gentle as he stroked the soft pink folds increasing her desire to a level of unrestrained excitement. She desperately needed more of him. His expert touch gave her a wonderful prelude to ecstasy.

Sensing she was ready, he moved his body above her. The warmth of his skin against hers was intoxicating and she felt the firmness of his arousal. He rubbed his erection against her, slowly at first, then her eager passion spurred him on. Thrilling her, he rhythmically slid the hard pulse of his arousal between her legs until every nerve-ending in her body was poised to explode. As he moved inside her, Ella felt involuntary tremors of pleasure that she had never experienced before. He moved in unison with her as passion surged through her veins. Shivers of delight overtook her. She soared more than once to an awesome shuddering frenzy of wild desire.

Looking into Ray's eyes revealing her excitement only seemed to make his own that much stronger. His eyes closed and she felt a burst of sensation unlike any other. Ray's mouth covered hers with a passionate kiss. "I love you, Ella," he managed to whisper just as he lost control. She loved how his breathing quickened and a muffled sound of delight erupted within him. As he convulsed with pure pleasure, Ella pulled him closer.

She had never been able to give herself, completely, to any man ~ until tonight. This was an erotic pleasure she had never known before. Slow, sensual, wild and raw, but beautiful, this was making love as she had never experienced. Ella felt an utter sense of completeness. The feeling was much more than sexual desire. It was love mixed with hunger as Ray caressed her afterward. He pulled the blanket from the back of the couch and wrapped them up in it. Ella felt as if she was in a cocoon of affection as she nestled her face against his hardened chest.

"Ella, I've never wanted any woman as much as I want you." Ray whispered as his lips brushed against her forehead.

Ella closed her eyes and smiled, "I feel the same way about you. I never believed in love at first sight, but now I do."

It was late evening when Ella convinced Ray to have something to eat in the kitchen. She handed him a robe and put hers on. While making a couple of sandwiches and having a beer, Ella couldn't stop smiling.

"You have a beautiful smile." Ray whispered as he took her hand in his across the table.

"I can't stop smiling." Ella said suddenly feeling self-conscious. "That was wild."

"I'm glad you liked it." Ray smiled, his eyes exuding mischief.

Ella giggled, "I really need to take a shower."

Ray continued smiling, "Go ahead, unless you want some company."

Ella's eyes met his and she took his hand. She turned on the hot water and her robe dropped to the floor. Ray's robe dropped even faster. He kissed her in the shower, then washed her hair. She soaped his body paying close attention to his masculine chest and taut abdomen. She felt him take her hand and he guided it to his erection. The hot water pulsed over them as she teased him.

Laughing, she shut off the water and they toweled off and brushed their teeth. Ella could see she was in for a treat. Ray chased her around the bed and tackled her gently. As her hair splayed around her he kissed her gently and said, "I've fallen for you."

Ella gazed into his eyes, "I know. I want you, Ray."

This time, she moved her hand down between his legs and stroked his shaft. She watched as his eyes closed with pleasure and a sound escaped from his lips, "Damn, that's good."

"I want to make you feel good, Ray." Ella was being bold. She had never been so forward with any man, but with Ray it felt right. She could be herself, uninhibited, for the first time and it felt wonderful. He made no demands upon her. There was no criticism or orders given. Ray was natural, relaxed, sexy, and he ignited something inside her that couldn't be described. It was primal, raw, unadulterated, and beautiful.

Ella sat up and faced Ray. His kiss was sweet and sexy. Her hand remained on his erection and she gently stroked him, slowly at first. She pushed him back upon the pillows and leaned down to caress him with her mouth. He gasped as her lips surrounded the sensitive head. She used her tongue to tantalize him.

Surprisingly, Ella found herself becoming aroused. No longer did she feel timid or shy about pleasuring Ray. His shaft was engorged and pulsing as she stopped and straddled him. He inhaled sharply as she mounted, then moved in a way that gave her great pleasure. She pleasured herself over and over and felt she could not stop if she wanted to.

CHAPTER 12

~ Bob ~

Bob decided he'd give Ella *one more chance* before he pulled out all of the stops to destroy Ray Adriano. He dialed her cell phone after driving by her beach house, but it went to voicemail. He knew she probably saw his number, recognized it, and decided not to answer her phone.

He figured he would try again tomorrow morning. But when she didn't pick up, he decided to drive by the beach house one more time. Maybe he would catch her in the yard with the puppy. She could have gone into work early. Maybe she was with clients at a real estate showing. But, then again, maybe she was purposefully ignoring him. He hoped it wasn't what he was thinking, but he couldn't get the thought out of his mind. It was only 8 AM, but he was driving down the street by her beach house as he spied the vintage Cadillac in the driveway. He instantly remembered the photo of it on Ella's Facebook page. *Ray Adriano was with her already.*

Bob felt his blood pressure rise as he dialed the number of Seth Bailey. His words were sharp and deliberate when he heard Seth pick up, "Hey. I've got something for you. Stop by the usual place in thirty minutes." Seth said he would and the phone call ended.

By the time Bob arrived at the park, the terrible feeling in the pit of his stomach intensified. Ella was already with Ray Adriano. *How could this have happened so quickly?*

Bob strolled along the interior of the park and found the empty bench. He sat for a moment browsing through the newspaper, then folded it and laid it on the bench. Five minutes later he walked back to the Mercedes and drove away.

As Seth approached the park bench in the city park, he sat down and casually picked up the newspaper. Inside the newspaper the address was written in block letters: *29 Beach Avenue, Rough Point. Vintage Cadillac.*

Bob was waiting in traffic for a red light, but at this angle could see Seth Bailey as he shuffled in his seat and tossed stale bread to the pigeons. In the middle of the newspaper he knew Seth discovered the usual payment and next to the money the note he had written: *I want it done as soon as possible.*

Standing up and looking in the opposite direction, Seth strolled out of the park, got into the small black Nissan and drove away. Bob was aware there were cameras everywhere these days but imagined even if he was observed, no one would suspect he'd even had contact with Seth Bailey.

Although his plan was set into motion, Bob wouldn't rest easy until he heard the news that Ray Adriano was gone. The low-life attorney was not going to remain in Ella's life, not if he could prevent it ~ and he knew he could. He was a man who let nothing stand in his way when he wanted something. And, he wanted Ella. He was always the winner, even if he had to bend the rules or eliminate them altogether ~ being the winner was the only thing that mattered.

He marveled at how quickly Ella lost interest in him the moment this attorney came along. Famous for his ability to win any client over in a business deal, Bob wondered why he couldn't win over Ella. She was no different than any other human being ~ she had a set of needs that had to be met and he could meet them. He would work his magic on her and win her back within a day or two.

As he thought of Ella making love with Ray Adriano he felt as if he would vomit. It was much worse than he originally thought. He couldn't focus on work when he got back to his office. At first he imagined that Ray Adriano was chasing Ella. But what if it was the other way around? What if Ella was tempting him, seducing him? The thought made him furious.

~ Ray ~

A sliver of sunlight woke him at 6:00 AM. As he opened his eyes, Ray turned toward Ella as she lay sleeping. Her hair was messy and her lips parted as she rhythmically inhaled and exhaled softly. He moved ever so slightly, not wanting to wake her and slipped into the bathroom soundlessly. The bathroom window shade was open and he walked to the window to close it. As he did, he saw someone in the driveway moving near the Cadillac.

Naked, he moved into the bedroom and pulled his shirt and pants on and scrambled to the front porch, trying to remain quiet. A small Nissan pulled away and drove recklessly until it was out of the neighborhood. It was black and the license plate was obscured, but Ray thought it started with B25. He walked outside into the cool crisp autumn air. Walking around the Cadillac he didn't notice anything out of place. But as he moved toward the house he caught something white on the ground near the edge of the driveway.

As he approached, he noticed it was simply the remains of a cigarette, the white filter. Instinctively, he walked into the house and found a plastic bag in the kitchen drawer and borrowed Ella's tweezers from her vanity. He walked back outside and picked the small piece of cotton and paper up with the tweezers and dropped it into the plastic bag and sealed it.

As he walked back inside, Ella stood in the bedroom doorway wrapped in a white cotton robe. "Hey. Good morning, Ray…" she said in a sexy sultry voice. "What are you doing outside?"

"Just looking for something in my car." Ray said, not wanting to alarm her. He moved across the room with lightning speed and embraced her, nuzzling her neck. No one on earth looked this good upon awakening in the morning.

"I need to brush my teeth." Ella giggled as he tickled her neck with kisses.

"Okay, you can, but come back to bed. I have something for you." Ray said with a devilish smile.

Ella smiled and disappeared into the bathroom. He listened to the water running and removed his clothing and slipped beneath the sheets, inhaling the warm sweet smell of Ella. Waiting for what seemed like twenty minutes, Ray closed his eyes and imagined what he was going to do with her. Everything about Ella excited him from the tip of her nose to the tip of her toes. And, he was aroused just thinking about holding her.

As she came through the doorway of the bedroom it was as if Ray was having a pleasant dream. Ella slipped beneath the covers without a stitch of clothing on and he kissed her soft lips, gently at first, but he was breathing heavily in her ear a few minutes later. Her hands explored his chest, and her fingers traced a line down his back. Her hands grasped his rear and she guided his arousal to just the right place, then she took him slowly, sensually, deliberately driving him wild. Making love in the morning was the ultimate pleasure for Ray. Hungrily, he relished every kiss, every touch, every moment with Ella as the sun highlighted her beautiful naked form sprawled upon the white bed sheet. She was his sex goddess and he, her willing subject.

Saying goodbye to Ray in the driveway, Ella promised she'd meet him at the designated spot late Friday afternoon on her drive to New York City. In the meantime, Ray had done the appraisal on the beach house and disbursed a check from her account to arrive via courier to the Andersons in California. Everything was all set for Ella to meet with Marina ~ the mystery woman her father loved so much.

Ella bristled with anticipation as she thought of the coming weekend. Ray insisted she stay at his apartment. He had secured a parking space for her, which was so sweet. As Ella walked into the real estate office her phone vibrated. She looked down and was surprised it was Ray.

His voice on the phone was serious and almost didn't sound like him, but she could tell he was trying to maintain his composure, "Ella, I don't want to worry you but I've been in an accident. The Cadillac got sideswiped."

Ella was filled with alarm, "What about you? Are you all right?"

"I got banged up, but luckily I swerved enough to avoid what could've been a really bad collision. The police are insisting that I go to the hospital to get an X-ray. I didn't want to worry you. I'll be all right. I had to let you know." Ray replied.

"Which hospital?" Ella asked.

"Eastern Maine." Ray uttered, sounding distracted, "Hey baby, I gotta go."

The phone went dead. Many images whirled through Ella's mind at once. She remembered her father's car accident only weeks ago. The phone call from Ray brought back all of the horrible feelings of that day. She told her secretary she'd be at the hospital and jumped into her vehicle.

When she arrived at Eastern Maine, Ray was already in the imaging center. No one was allowed in, so she waited in the outer office. She practiced deep breathing to steady her nerves and drank a bottle of water. She watched the minutes tick by on the huge wall clock. What was taking so long?

Finally, Ray emerged from the imaging area. He saw her and she ran to him.

"What's going on? Tell me." Ella begged.

"A lot of bruising, nothing broken." Ray grimaced in pain as he put his jacket on.

"What happened?" Ella queried, "Did someone cut you off or run into you?"

"The brakes failed." Ray said gazing at her. "They felt a little spongy when I started out, but when I got to the on-ramp for the highway the pedal went straight to the floor. I couldn't stop the vehicle, even the parking brake didn't work. I was traveling at a fairly high rate of speed, maybe forty miles an hour and, wham! Another vehicle collided right into me as I was merging onto the interstate. They're towing the car to a restoration shop nearby. Hopefully, they can repair it."

Ella embraced him. "Come home with me."

"Actually, I'll take a ride to get a rental car. I need to get back to the city. Lots to do there." Ray smiled. "I'll be all right. Really."

Gingerly, Ray got into Ella's car and she drove him to the nearest car rental franchise and within a few minutes he had a Lexus warming up in the parking lot.

Ray stood in the parking lot embracing Ella for a good long time. When he kissed her she felt her knees go weak. She didn't want him to go. Now that she knew what it was like to be with him, she couldn't imagine her life without him. She knew she would think about him until she saw him again. Some girls were hooked on chocolate, her addiction had become Ray Adriano.

"I'll miss you, baby." He whispered into her ear.

"I wish you didn't have to go." Ella whispered back.

Ray called his office but the moment Blake heard what happened, he began asking questions about the details of the accident. Ray told him everything that he knew. "The brake fluid was all over the road and the policemen knew right away the brakes had failed. They took photos to reconstruct the scene."

The next sentence Blake uttered made Ray almost stop breathing.

"That's exactly the way Ella's father died. The brakes failed on his vintage car. He drove an old Buick, 1948, I think. Kept the thing in tip-top shape. When the police did the forensics at the scene, they towed the car to a garage up in Maine, I can't remember the name of it, but the mechanic at the garage said *someone cut the brake line purposefully.* Get in touch with the Portland Police. Let me see, I have the detective's card here somewhere…" Blake was fumbling in his desk.

Taking Blake's advice, within minutes Ray was heading into downtown Portland and parked in the visitor's slot. He jogged up the stairs into the building that looked more like a fortress than a police station. He had to pass through several bulletproof reception areas until he was escorted to a small room where he waited to hear from Detective Sanchez. The door buzzed and Sanchez entered the interrogation room. He was probably in his late 30's, medium build, dark haired, and looked Ray squarely in the eye.

"How can I help you, sir?" Sanchez asked.

Ray explained the details of the accident, but more importantly asked to see the accident report for John Wakefield's recent collision. "What's the name of the garage restoring Mr. Wakefield's vehicle?"

"Willy's, they're the best." Sanchez grinned. "I have an old 1955 myself."

But Sanchez was now comparing the two reports and asked Ray to ride with him to pay a visit to Willy's. As they got into the undercover detective's vehicle, Sanchez continued talking, "We need details. These two accidents are too similar to be coincidence. Who would've wanted John Wakefield dead? And, who would've wanted you out of the picture? Do you have any enemies, Mr. Adriano?"

"I don't know how to say this, but I do know of one guy who'd probably like to rip out my throat right about now." Ray uttered, "Bob Albertson."

"Why would he want to do that?" Sanchez probed.

"Because I'm sleeping with his girlfriend, ex-girlfriend." Ray whispered.

"And you think this guy would be so pissed off he'd want to kill you?" Sanchez asked.

"It's possible." Ray continued. "She's an heiress, worth millions. He was extremely upset when she walked out on him."

"Have you noticed anything strange in the last few days leading up to the accident? Has this Bob made any threatening gestures, phone calls, or has he called you?" Sanchez asked.

"No, but I did notice someone this morning near my car. Or, at least I thought I saw someone. It was early, I had just awakened and pulled on my clothes. It was a black Nissan, I only caught a glimpse, the plate started with B25, I think. Oh, and I found this in the driveway." Ray fished out the plastic baggie with the cigarette butt inside.

"Very nice." Sanchez smiled at him. "You've just given me a lot of information that could be enough to get us a lead." Sanchez got on the phone and called the station with the information Ray had just given him.

Pulling into Willy's reminded Ray of stepping back into the 1940's. The place was old, probably built during World War Two, and the proprietor was about the same vintage. Although he'd be considered elderly, Willy Stanton was sharp and witty. He was in the doorway of his shop as their car pulled into the driveway. "Can I help you, boys?"

Sanchez and Ray got out of the vehicle. "That's mine you're working on." Ray smiled.

Ray felt Willy's eyes on him as he sized him up, "Somebody want you dead?"

"That's the second time I've been asked that question today." Ray answered.

"Well, this brake line was brand spanking new. Someone used a cutting tool to cause it to fail, and they knew what they were doing. They cut it just enough so all of the brake fluid wouldn't come out at once. This was planned, gentlemen." Willy ran his hand through what was left of his gray hair. "Saw one just like it a few weeks ago. John Wakefield's '48, God rest his soul. He was a great guy."

Sanchez took photos of the undercarriage of the vehicle while it was up on the lift. Willy filled out paperwork distinctly stating that the brake line was cut. He also filled out paperwork stating the same about John Wakefield's 1948 Buick. The two men rode back to the station. "What should I do?" Ray asked Sanchez, hoping he understood the question.

"Do you carry?" Sanchez asked.

"Yes, I do. But I don't have a permit." Ray answered.

"You can apply for one and I can have it expedited. Are you clean?" Sanchez asked.

"As a whistle." Ray replied.

"Fill out the form at the station. I'll do my best to get it approved. In the meantime, carry it, and be ready to think outside of the box. Someone wants you dead, Mr. Adriano, and when someone sets their mind to it ~ you can be gone in a split second. Watch your back." Sanchez warned. "In the meantime, let's get this cigarette to forensics. I'll need to get a DNA sample from Bob Albertson."

~ Ella ~

She had several real estate appointments but her mind was on Ray for the rest of the day. She was surprised when her phone vibrated and it was him explaining his day-long adventure with Detective Sanchez.

"We need to get a DNA sample from Bob Albertson. I don't have any idea yet how to accomplish that. I'll be at your place in five minutes."

Ella was excited and happy to have Ray staying at the beach house. She now wondered if Bob had something to do with the brakes failing on his car. It was completely possible. Even more horrifying was the thought that Bob had arranged her father's death. She swallowed hard at the thought of that. Could it be possible she was living with the man who murdered her father, or at least had him killed?

She wracked her brain thinking of how to get a DNA sample, then it suddenly occurred to her. When she packed her bathroom things to move, she had scooped toothpaste and toothbrushes from the vanity into a box. When she took her toothbrush out of the box, she noticed one in there that belonged to Bob. She distinctly remembered tossing it into the wastebasket in the bathroom and she ran in and retrieved it with a tissue and put it into a plastic baggie.

When Ray came to the door, she embraced him, "I have Bob's DNA on a toothbrush." She smiled. "Good, we need to get that to Sanchez."

As Ray turned to get back into his vehicle, Ella noticed a car pulling up in front of the house and a solid dark-haired man jumped out. Ray shook detective Sanchez's hand and introduced him to Ella. "Here's Bob Albertson's DNA." Ray handed him the toothbrush in the bag.

"Come inside and sit down," Sanchez spoke softly. "I ran the plate you gave me. A few cameras picked up some activity on that vehicle."

Within a few minutes, Sanchez explained the vehicle belonged to Seth Bailey. Ray and Ella said they never heard the name. But Sanchez continued, "Seth Bailey was seen in the park downtown and cameras photographed him in this neighborhood shortly after that. Cameras also captured the Mercedes owned by Bob Albertson in the area of the park. The two are connected somehow."

"Oh my God," Ella blurted, "These guys killed my father, and now they're trying to kill Ray?"

"We don't *know* that for a fact, Ma'am." Sanchez spoke softly. "But, it's under investigation, and I would suggest you assume the worst, just in case. Take extra precautions and be aware of your surroundings."

~ Bob ~

Infuriated that Ray Adriano wasn't dead, but back at Ella's now driving a Lexus, he wanted the money back that he'd given to Seth Bailey. The stupid kid didn't do the job he was paid to do. Bob paced back and forth as he waited for Seth to arrive at the Donut Express. Several customers stared at him and moved away. He hated being seen in a donut shop. Had he really sunk to this?

The door swung open and Seth moved to the corner table. "What do you want?"

"I want to talk with you, outside." Bob hissed at him through clenched teeth.

Seth slid into the Mercedes and Bob unleashed his rage, "You idiot. There was a job to be done and you failed. I got ripped off. I want the money back."

"No refunds." Seth replied. "But if you give me more, I can guarantee it this time."

"You little bastard. You think you can order me around like you're in charge? Bob lost his composure and people in the parking lot stared. He took a deep breath to steady himself.

"Let's get this straight," Bob locked the car doors remotely and grabbed Seth by the throat, "I don't hand money to losers who can't get the job done." Seth struggled beneath his grasp. Bob felt he could have continued and choked him right there, but he wasn't worth the trouble. Instead, he released his grip and waited as Seth rubbed his neck.

"You're crazy, man." Seth coughed.

Bob handed Seth Bailey an envelope with more money and leaned close to his face. "Get it done this time, or I'm coming after you." Bob said in a threatening tone.

"Yeah, right." Seth uttered with disdain. The Mercedes unlocked and Seth exited the vehicle and drove away.

Bob couldn't believe how stupid this kid was. He was giving him thousands in cash and he couldn't complete one simple task. No wonder he was at the bottom of the food chain. He was an idiot. This time, Bob assumed the extra money would guarantee Ray Adriano's demise. He knew Seth had guns, many of them, and he was proficient in the use of them. Why didn't he just shoot Ray Adriano from a distance and get it over with? These types of murders went unsolved every day.

He drove to his office in a state of anger, filled with angst. He had to call Ella and tell her he loved her. Maybe she'd take his call or maybe not. Better yet, he would stop by the real estate office and be particularly sweet. He'd send her flowers first. He knew if he persisted, she'd eventually come back to him and bring her fortune with her.

The one thing he had going for him was that Ray Adriano was a loser. He was a failure of a human being, and would never be able to give Ella the lifestyle that he could provide. He had to worm his way back into Ella's heart somehow. He remembered the first few dates they had and how much she seemed to like him ~ she loved him. But, she was giving her love to a low-life nobody now and he set his teeth with determination. No one ever stopped Bob Albertson from obtaining what he wanted – no one.

CHAPTER 13

~ Ray ~

The night with Ella was a bonus he hadn't planned on. They cooked dinner together and watched television like a married couple. Ray was in awe of Ella's grace and poise in the midst of this crisis. The plan for her to meet Marina in New York was still in play. She spoke about going to New York excitedly. Ray knew it would be good to get out of the area, especially if Bob was tracking her.

Ray had his revolver in his bag, just in case there was trouble. Instinctively, he knew Bob Albertson was behind what happened to Ella's father and the attempt on his life. He would like nothing more than to beat the bastard to a bloody pulp. But he reined in his anger and focused on Ella tonight.

The day had been filled with stress and unexpected news. Ray wanted Ella to feel safe and comfortable, as much as she could in light of the events of the day. He watched as she reclined on the sofa. Ray took Boomer outside for his after-dinner romp. Boomer jumped around in the small fenced-in yard in an attempt to get Ray to play with him. Ray rolled a small ball around in the yard for a while but the sun was slipping toward the horizon and darkness crept over them.

Inside, he sat with Ella on the sofa. She instantly curled herself against him, her head rested upon his chest. He thought for a moment if he was going to spend the last night of his life alive, he wanted it to be with Ella, like this. His hand brushed her hair aside and he placed his soft kiss on her forehead. He wanted to be her respite from the painful events of the day.

"Oh, Ray, I'm afraid." She whispered.

"I'm taking you to New York with me." He consoled her. "Sanchez is a good detective. He will get to the bottom of this. We need to trust him."

Sleeping with Ella was heavenly. He left on a few lights and checked all of the windows and doors to put her fears to rest. He put the revolver on the nightstand. Snuggling together, he listened to her breathing become regular as she fell into a deep sleep. But Ray stayed awake wondering if Bob was behind all of this. A flash of defiance ran through him.

In the morning, Willy called him and said he had sourced the parts for the brakes on the Cadillac. He promised the body work would be done with the greatest of precision.

Ray kept the rental Lexus and spirited Ella to New York City early the next morning. Stopping for lunch along the way and giving Boomer an opportunity to run around, the trip was leisurely and enjoyable. Arriving in the city, he pulled into the parking spot in the garage. He told Ella he wanted to take her to a nice little Italian restaurant which was a short walk from his apartment.

Boomer sniffed the sidewalks of New York as if a smorgasbord of smells were contained there. Ray brought Ella up the three flights of stairs and through the series of bolts and locks to his hidden one-room apartment. At least it was a big room. Rosa had performed a small miracle cleaning and painting and adding new furniture. Ray opened the door and Ella gasped, "It's beautiful, Ray!" She ran to the window to enjoy the view of the East River.

Ray sat on the brand new sofa and beckoned her to sit beside him. "I have dinner planned for tonight, then early in the morning I want to take you to the Empire State Building. Would you like that?"

Ella smiled. "Oh sure. I'd love to go to the Empire State Building. And, the Statue of Liberty, too."

Ray suspected she'd been to those places in the past. "You're just being nice, aren't you?" he queried.

"Actually, I could skip those two. I've been to see them several times, and I think they are beautiful." Ella confessed.

"What would you like to do?" Ray asked her.

"I'd like to go to the bar where you worked weekends. I want to know more about you." Ella's request stunned him. Who really wanted to know about his boring workaholic life in New York? She did.

"Okay, after we have the meeting with Marina tomorrow morning, I will take you to Tony's for lunch." Ray couldn't believe he was uttering those words, but he would do whatever Ella wanted, even this.

Dinnertime was fast approaching and Ella squeezed herself into Ray's tiny bathroom and managed to wash up and change. She chose a soft purple cashmere sweater over a lilac cotton shirt. Comfortable black pants and boots completed her simple outfit. After slicking on a nude shimmery lipstick, Ella left her hair free and pulled loose strands back with a barrette. As she stepped out of the bathroom, she was surprised to notice Ray had gotten dressed and shaved in the kitchen.

"How do I look?" Ella smiled as she twirled in the middle of the room. Ray furrowed his brow and frowned. "I don't know, Ella. There seems to be something missing."

Ella seemed a little surprised by his answer. But she smiled when he handed her a small box and he watched as she opened it with child-like wonder, then squealed. She fingered the pair of breathtakingly beautiful diamond earrings in the box. "Oh gosh!" she whispered.

Pops had given them to him a year ago. He knew they'd look perfect on Ella. Ray loved to see her smile and he loved her voice when she asked, "Ray, how did you *know* I love diamond earrings?"

"Just a guess." He laughed. "They do look stunning on you. His hand touched one of the earrings as it dangled in the light. "But It's *you* that makes them look beautiful."

He kissed Ella's lips lightly and took her hand. "Come on, we can walk to dinner from here."

~Ella~

Ella was happy that she wore comfortable shoes. She noticed women in New York wore three-inch heels, some maybe higher than that. She could never walk at a brisk pace with those things on, not to mention how much they probably deformed the human foot.

Ray stopped in front of an old brownstone building that looked more like someone's home. The doorman ushered them in and announced their name softly to the Maitre'd, "Adriano, sir."

Ella had never imagined her last name being the same as Ray's but it had a nice ring to it, *Ella Adriano*. She smiled at the Maitre'd and they were whisked to a private table in the corner of the room. Candles were lit, fresh flowers filled the room with a delightful fresh aroma.

"The menu is written there on the blackboard in Italian." Ray informed her. "I can read it to you, just tell me what you like." Ray proceeded to speak Italian, then translated to English. She was hypnotized by his command of the language. About halfway through, she stopped him, "I want chicken…that dish you just said." Ella giggled.

Dinner was delicious and Ella savored every bite. But even more, she savored every moment with Ray. He ordered dessert to go as the evening was still early.

"Would you take me to Tony's tonight?" she asked softly as they arrived back in his apartment. She noticed Ray hesitated, then he gave in. He put dessert in the refrigerator and took her hand. They walked a few blocks in the opposite direction then turned down a shorter street. The neon sign simply said, Tony's. The place appeared to be packed with people even at 8:30 PM.

"I don't want to stay long." Ray said as they approached. "It gets a little wild in here on Friday nights."

He'd rather have his fingernails ripped out one-by-one than take Ella into Tony's. The moment he walked in the doorway with her, he was greeted with a chorus of wolf whistles and cat calls. Every head turned as he walked Ella to the bar and asked her what she wanted to drink. He introduce her to the waitresses and the bartenders. Every employee turned to look at Ella. A guy sitting on a bar stool moved and gave his seat to Ella.

"Where the hell have you been, Ray?" Vanessa was suddenly at his side. Her hand with the long fancy fingernails touched the back of his head and he felt himself smiling awkwardly. "Vanessa, I'd like you to meet Ella Wakefield."

He watched as Ella took Vanessa in. Of more concern was the way Vanessa chewed her bubblegum and snapped it while she gawked at Ella. Always the lady, Ray watched as Ella smiled warmly, or at least pretended to. But he could tell by the look in her eyes that Vanessa was not a person she wanted in her presence.

Ray inserted himself between the two women and decided to take control, "I have been in Maine working with Ella on her father's estate. I had a little fender-bender while there and, well, one thing led to another. Ella is here in the city to finish some business."

"Yeah, monkey business." Sam, one of the bartenders said it, and everyone laughed. Ray hoped that was the only wise ass comment that would be made, but he knew it was probably wasn't. Most likely there would be more to come.

Ella had a tall Sam Adams ale in front of her. She glanced at Ray, "This is fine."

The bartender, Sam, was already flirting with Ella. He was asking way too many questions and couldn't take his eyes off her, which only served to piss off Ray. Ella politely laughed at Sam's lame jokes, even the one where he told Ella that Sam Adams beer was named after him.

Tony came down from his office to say hello to Ray ~ well, he surmised that Tony really wanted to say hello to Ella ~ and he was right.

"Where has he been keeping you? Ella, is it?" Tony extended his hand and Ella shook it flashing a perfect smile. Tony overtly ogled her which made Ray squirm.

"Really, Tony, don't you have some work to do in your office upstairs?" Ray wise-cracked.

"No, I think I will stay down here and enjoy the scenery." Tony responded with a wink and a smile.

Vanessa was back, even though she had tables filled with customers waiting. "So, what are you two doing tonight, Ray? Will you take Ella back to your lair?" She snapped her gum and her blonde ponytail swung toward him. "His apartment is really something, Ella, but the view of the river is nice, especially in the moonlight."

Ella smiled but when Vanessa walked away, Ray was at a loss for words. Several of his friends came over to the bar and stood next to Ella. Oh no, his law school friends, Rick, Rob, and Miles.

"Where are you from, Ella?" Rick asked.

"We didn't know Ray had a *real* girlfriend." Rob said with a smile.

The shy one, Miles, just stared at Ella. Then he grinned and gestured, "Why don't you come and sit with us?"

Ray seemed unable to stop the tsunami of people who wanted to say hello to Ella and stick their nose into his business. Red-faced, he slunk into the booth with Ella and his friends. Rick and Rob continued asking her questions and Miles just drooled on himself.

Graciously, Ella answered everything they asked. Then, she adroitly turned the questions to them. She only had to make one request and it got them all chattering at once, "So, tell me about Ray."

Not that he had anything in his past to be nervous about, but he hated to be the subject of discussion at Tony's on a crowded Friday night. God knew what some of these people might say, especially Vanessa. He was trying every evasion tactic known to man to stay out of her line of vision. But she honed in on him like a laser beam and walked right up to the table. "So, what does my Ray-Ray want tonight?" her voice sounded like fingernails on a chalkboard all of a sudden.

Ray smiled sheepishly and said, "Ray has to go to the men's room."

He escaped from the table and couldn't believe Vanessa was following him. She could be pushy sometimes, but this was going over the line. She caught his arm just before he made it through the doorway to the men's room. Guys were bumping into him and he stepped aside. "Vanessa, will you just get lost tonight, please?" Ray made his appeal.

"Where'd you pick her up?" Vanessa was not letting him off the hook.

"She's a client. Ella is actually here in the city on business this weekend." He said, trying to sound professional.

"Yeah, she's here on business all right…" Vanessa glared at him, "funny business."

"Look, Vanessa, I don't want to have this conversation right now. Please…go wait on tables, flirt with guys ~ do whatever it is that you do…but lay off Ella." Ray said somberly.

Vanessa turned on her heel with her blonde ponytail swaying back and forth. Her exaggerated hip movement was dramatic, nothing but a disgusting display of drama. He kicked himself for ever taking her to his apartment. But he knew Ella picked up on it.

He hoped Vanessa would steer clear of the table. He used the men's room and hastily got back. God only knew what the others had said to Ella while he was gone for all of five minutes.

The guys were all laughing at something Ella had said. She seemed to have them in the palm of her hand, entertaining them with stories of the trip to the fishing camp. When Ray got back into the booth, he sat on the end and smiled at Ella. She seemed to be having a good time. Vanessa only walked by twice, but her stare let him know what she was thinking. Ray couldn't get out of Tony's quickly enough that night.

Ella was gracious and allowed Ray to bow out gently, telling the gang they had someplace to go. Whatever he said, Ella went along with it and as soon as they were outside walking in the cool night air, Ray thanked her.

"I'm sorry you had to run that gauntlet, Ella." Ray felt he owed her an apology. He knew Tony's wasn't the type of place someone like Ella would frequent.

"Please don't say that." Ella slipped her arm around his. "I had a good time, in fact, it gave me a little peek into your life. Your friends spoke highly of you. And, it seems Vanessa is an admirer of yours."

~ Ella ~

Back at the apartment, Ella took Boomer on a walk around the block before turning in for the night and Ray held her hand while walking. A sweet gesture, really so simple, but it comforted her.

Ella imagined that Ray might have had someone clean his apartment because it was spotless and the bed had rose petals sprinkled in and around it. The tiny lamp on the dresser cast a golden glow barely illuminating Ray as he stood in the doorway watching Ella undress. It was the first time she had ever disrobed with a man staring at her. In her mind, she made it into a game, of sorts, to see who would break eye contact first.

Ray's eyes held hers as she removed her sweater, then her shirt, and by the time she unbuttoned her pants, he was embracing her. "Oh babe, I can't wait." he whispered in her ear.

"I don't want you to wait." She whispered back. His lips found hers and he kissed her sweetly. In Ella's mind, Ray could write a book about kissing. He knew exactly how to touch his lips to hers causing her to ache for him. Starting out slowly, he built to a crescendo ending with a sensuous French kiss that made her knees weak.

"Damn, you know how to kiss," she murmured. His mouth dropped to her neck and he placed a warm caress just beneath her ear. He knew where her erogenous zones were, and he worked them like an expert. As Ella reclined on the bed, Ray took his shirt off. The smirk on his face said all she needed to know. She reached for his waistband and whispered, "Let me do this."

Slowly, she unbuttoned his pants, then unzipped and she could tell he was like a racehorse at the starting gate. As she slid his pants down, she worked at his boxer-brief underwear, giggling when she saw Sponge Bob on them. "I have to ask…" she teased him.

"If you must know, they were a secret Santa gift. Hey, they fit, so I wear them." Ray smiled. Ella had to admire a guy secure enough to wear those. But Ray was like that. He didn't have anything to prove. The underwear ended up on the floor and Ella's laughter turned to something else. Longing, desire, lust, call it what you want ~ she was experiencing all of those feelings and more as she gazed at Ray's erection in the bedroom.

He got into the bed and laid against the pillows and she sensed Ray knew she was mesmerized as she gazed upon his naked form. The aroma of the rose petals mixed with his cologne was delicious. As he French kissed her with precision, her hand wandered to the place she knew he wanted her to touch. She wondered for a moment if she could ever get enough of him. It was wild, really. Touching Ray, feeling his excitement, letting herself get swept away with the instinctual pleasure of it all.

The kissing, the touching, the gentle foreplay brought Ella to a place she had never been. This must be what her girlfriends were talking about when they discussed the best sex they'd ever had. She had read somewhere that every person has a perfect partner out there somewhere and when that connection was made, no one else would suffice. Ella felt Ray was hers.

CHAPTER 14

~ Ray ~

Morning came too quickly. What a night it had been. All of the hopes and dreams he had about Ella had come true. He had sprawled atop his bed many nights wondering what it would be like to hold her and make love to her in his apartment. Now she was with him, in his bed sound asleep. He felt he had to pinch himself. It could all be a wonderful dream.

He slipped quietly into the shower and cleaned up for the pending meeting with Marina. He called the doorman to his office building reminding him that Marina would be arriving at 9:00 AM and to have someone escort her to the private elevator that went directly to his office. He heard Ella stirring in the bedroom.

"I'll take the dog outside, Ella." He said as he kissed her sweet lips.

"Thank you, so much." She mumbled. Her hair was disheveled and eyes half-closed but he found Ella to be most beautiful in the morning just awakening. Self-consciously, she wrapped herself in his robe and trekked toward the bathroom. She turned and smiled at him taking his breath away. Just before he closed the door to take Boomer out to the hallway, he said, "There's hot coffee on the counter for you."

He locked every door and made his way down the three flights to the street. Boomer was happy to be outside. His nose was busy sniffing every inch of the sidewalk. Ray found a patch of green grass and brought the dog to it. Once back inside, Ray freshened the puppy's water bowl and fed him. While Ella got dressed, Ray played with Boomer on the floor. A dog lover, Ray's heart melted every time he held the pup.

When Ella appeared in the kitchen, Ray thought she looked particularly gorgeous. But she seemed oblivious to her own beauty. Ella's hair was in a ponytail and she was wearing a T-shirt, a long cotton cardigan and jeans. "Do you think this is too casual?" She turned to him.

"No, in fact, I think you look comfortable." Ray replied, wanting to kiss her again, but he didn't want to smear her lipstick. "Ready to go?" he asked.

"Yes, I'm ready." Ella's eyes locked with his. He sensed she was nervous.

"I've met her, Ella. She seems really nice. I don't mean phony-nice and polite. I mean she is down-home nice." Ray elaborated. "She struck me as a genuine, no frills, honest type of person."

"I hope she likes me." Ella said as they walked downstairs to the street.

Ray turned to her just before he unlocked the door to the outside. "She will love you."

As he opened the heavy steel door and locked it, a multitude of smells assaulted his senses. Street vendor food, car exhaust, the lingering smell of motor oil which seemed to permeate every inch of the city. He walked along the street-side of the sidewalk with his arm around her. He was her protector as the city streets filled with pedestrians, dog-walkers, panhandlers, and those wandering aimlessly. The sound of traffic filled the air and within twenty minutes they were inside the hushed enclave of the law firm. Ray nodded to the doorman and stopped at the reception desk. "Hey, George. Has Miss Sokolova arrived yet?"

George nodded, "Yes sir, she came just a moment ago. I brought her to your conference room, as you instructed. There's food up there, too." Ray handed George some money and whisked Ella into the elevator. He could tell she was nervous and he kissed her in the elevator in an effort to distract her, but he really wanted the kiss for himself. He wondered how any man could go longer than an hour without kissing her. And, hoped she'd never tire of him doing so.

More than anything, he wanted Ella to have a positive meeting with Marina Sokolova. He felt this would give her some closure on her father's death. There was so much brewing in that pretty head of Ella's, and he only had a kernel of knowledge about any of it.

Ray opened the conference room door and Marina was standing there with her hair in a ponytail, wearing a T-shirt, a cardigan and a pair of well-worn jeans. Her smile was genuine. If she was wearing make-up, it was undetectable except for the shimmery lipstick. He watched as her eyes took in Ella, the dark beauty standing next to him.

"Ella, my dear, it's so good to meet you." Marina spoke softly and extended her hand as they approached.

Ella's voice was soft and professional, "It's wonderful to meet you, Marina."

Ray seated the two women on the sofa in the conference room and asked the obvious question, "Would either of you like coffee or tea?" He served them tea and fruit and slipped away as he heard them begin a lively conversation.

She was looking into the face of Marina Sokolova. Ella was staring even though she knew it was rude, but she couldn't believe her eyes. Marina was beautiful. Not just model-perfect as on the cover of magazines; she had beauty that emanated from within. A positive energy radiated from her eyes the moment they met. Ella immediately felt at ease.

Marina started talking first, "I've wanted to meet you for many years. Your father loved you so much, Ella. He spoke of you often. You were the light of his life. You're a brave young woman to request this meeting. I know it must be difficult for you. You must miss him terribly." Marina shattered all of the pre-conceived notions Ella held about her all these years. She wasn't only beautiful but she was gracious and kind.

"I've known about you for many years, too." Ella said swallowing hard. "My father finally told me when I was in high school why he left my mother. Maybe he told me because I pestered him so much. I guessed he had a lover. But when I found out it was you, I have to admit I was shocked."

"He was a kind man, your father." Marina continued, "He became wealthy but he didn't allow that to change him. He continued to be a man who was pleased with simple things. He loved fishing and golfing, just being outdoors. I have many wonderful memories, Ella, and I'd like to share them with you if you'd be comfortable with that."

"Sure." Ella smiled, "I'd love to hear about your life with him. Every time someone talks about him, it makes me feel like he's still alive. Of course, he always will be in my heart."

"Then you may like to see these." Marina pulled a photo album out of a large box sitting on the floor next to the sofa. "I have many photographs. I loved modeling, but my true love was photography. I photograph models now, in fact, and enjoy being behind the lens instead of in front of it."

Ella delicately opened the photo album, almost afraid to open it for fear she may cry. The first photograph, however, captured her attention. It was her father at the fishing camp wearing a flannel shirt. That was how Ella remembered him. As she flipped each page slowly, Ella scrutinized every photograph. Marina was definitely a talented photographer. She captured the very essence of John Wakefield in every picture. Several photos were of Marina and her father together. They looked so much in love, like a newly married couple.

For two hours, Marina answered Ella's questions and told her stories about her life with John Wakefield. Ella learned that her father lived in a Penthouse overlooking Central Park most of his life and traveled extensively when Marina went on photo shoots. There were photos from all over the world. Ella laughed at some of the funny stories. She knew they were true, because Marina knew every detail about him, his taste in food, in music, right down to his favorite television shows to watch.

Surprising her, Marina touched Ella's hand and whispered, "I had these albums made for you. I have a set. I want you to have these." Ella didn't know what to say. These photographs meant more to her than anything else Marina could have given her. She immediately felt the sting of tears in her eyes. She swallowed hard, "Thank you, Marina. You don't know how much I appreciate this."

Marina smiled. Ella could tell she was happy. "Tell me about your life, Ella. Are you engaged to Bob Albertson?"

Ella looked down. "No. I moved out of Bob's house two days ago. He's not the man for me."

"Really..." Marina said with relief. "I never liked Bob. That is one of the *only* arguments I ever had with your father."

"What do you mean?" Ella's eyes met hers and she intuitively felt there was more to that story.

"Bob Albertson was not a true friend to your father." Marina responded, "Trust me, I know. But, for some reason your father liked him. I found Bob Albertson to be a very manipulative person. He knew how to get what he wanted."

"How well did you know Bob?" Ella was filled with curiosity.

"He is the one who talked your father into making a trust for you; but in the same breath, Bob Albertson told your father he wanted to marry you. He wanted your father to make the marriage to him a stipulation of receiving your inheritance." Marina's face was serious.

Ella nearly stopped breathing for a moment. "But, my father wouldn't do that."

"You are right. *Your father refused to do so.* But I remember Bob was constantly pressuring him. He even had the paperwork drawn up. He tried to convince your father that he was the only one who could take care of you ~ and his fortune." Marina became silent.

"Marina," Ella said softly, "Do you still live here in New York?"

"Yes, I am here when I'm not doing a photo shoot on location." Marina replied.

"I'd like to have lunch with you sometime. Would you like that?" Ella ventured.

"Yes! I'd love it!" Marina said enthusiastically. "Here's my phone number and e-mail. You can text me when you're in town. You know, I'd love to go to that fishing camp sometime."

"Maybe you can come to Maine in the summer and we can go there!" Ella felt a surge of excitement. "It would be fun. We could go fishing. Dad's boat is still there. Everything is just as he left it."

"I'd love that, Ella." Marina smiled.

Ray popped his head into the conference room. "Your driver is here, Miss Sokolova," he announced.

"Please, call me Marina." She smiled. The two women stood simultaneously and Marina gave Ella a warm hug. "It was so good to meet you, Ella. You are every bit as delightful as I imagined."

"Thank you, Marina. I'll treasure these photos. I'm so glad I got to meet you." Ella said softly. And, Marina was gone. Ella imagined she was being swept away by her driver to her penthouse or maybe flying to another country for a location shoot. What an exciting woman! She was the complete opposite of Ella's mother. Which reminded her, she needed to stop and see her mother soon. She hadn't seen her since her father died, and even then it was an abbreviated visit.

Ray was at her side, "Are you all right?"

"Oh yes, I'm fine." Ella said, but she was deep in thought. The meeting with Marina gave her a lot to think about. So many unanswered questions were now obvious to Ella. The one thing that stayed with her was the comment about Bob and her father's trust.

"Ray, I have a question about my trust." Ella informed him.

"What?" Ray responded.

"Did my father add a clause that said I'd need to be married to Bob in order to receive my inheritance?" Ella said the words slowly.

"I didn't see anything like that in the paperwork." Ray said. "But my office is two doors down the hall; let's go in there and I'll get the file."

Ray went through the file. "Nothing like that." He said.

Just as he spoke, the courier knocked on his office door. "You've been away, Mr. Adriano, there's mail for you."

Ray took the stack of mail wrapped with rubber bands. "I'll just sift through this. Have a coffee. I'll only be a minute, then we'll leave."

Ella felt relieved there was no provision attached to her inheritance. She walked to the conference room and found a bottle of water. When she returned to Ray's office he was reading a piece of mail that arrived in a special delivery envelope. "Ella, you'd better sit down."

"What – what is it?" she asked with a sick feeling in her stomach.

"It's from your mother. A legal document, it's a codicil with your father's signature." Ray said slowly.

"What the hell is a codicil?" Ella asked abruptly.

But the look on Ray's face told her everything she needed to know. Ray motioned for her to sit, "A codicil is like an addition to a will…sort of a postscript…an add-on."

"What does it say?" Ella's hand was trembling and she suddenly couldn't breathe.

~ Ray ~

He didn't want to read the words before him, but he had to tell Ella. The codicil to John Wakefield's will spelled out the thing she feared the most: *In order to obtain her inheritance, she had to marry Bob Albertson.* She would get a $500,000 pay-out immediately, identical to what his wife and mistress received, but the rest of the fortune would be held in trust until she married Bob.

Ella looked like she was going to faint. "She said he'd never sign it! *Marina knew about this ~ she said my father refused to sign it!*" Ella cried. "Oh God, Ray, what do I do now?

Anger simmered in Ray as he read the words on the pages before him. "We can try to get this overturned; we can dispute it," Ray responded. "But, it could be a long battle. It appears to be a legal document. The signature appears to be that of your father. There's a witness signature. It has been notarized. But, we can contest it on the grounds that your father was under duress at the time…or, it's a forgery."

"How do we *prove* that?" Ella asked.

"I don't know yet." Ray tried to console her. "I need to dig into this. I don't want to disappoint you, but these things can be protracted, drawn out. Don't get discouraged." Tears formed in Ella's eyes and Ray rushed to embrace her. "There, now…" he said as he held her close to his chest. "Don't worry."

But he knew this was trouble. He wondered why this document was delayed and being sent to him now. There were too many questions and he had to find the answers. Ella needed him to be strong and confident, so that's what he projected. "Come on. Let's go to lunch. We can talk about this." Ray offered.

Finally she acquiesced, "Okay. Lunch. Yes, that sounds good."

Ray took Ella to his favorite pizza place in Little Italy. He even got her to smile once or twice. But he could tell by the look on her face she was preoccupied with the stipulation on her inheritance. He couldn't ignore the topic or try to gloss over it. "Ella, baby, listen. You've got $500,000. Invested properly, that will pay the mortgage on the beach house, or most of it. You have a job. You are young. You have time for me to fight this and win it. Please give me the chance." Ray implored.

"I've got to see my mother, like right away. There's something wrong with this picture." Ella said with defiance. "Marina said my father would never sign that document. We had a long talk about this. She told me she never trusted Bob. That's the one thing she argued with my father about."

"I'm going with you." Ray whispered. "I want to get to the bottom of this, too."

"We need to leave tonight. I'm going to drop-in unannounced." Ella said. "I don't want to give mother time to prepare a response to what I'm going to say."

Within an hour, Ray was whisking Ella out of the city in the darkness heading north.

"It was mailed two days ago." Beth Wakefield told Bob as he stood in her kitchen drumming his fingers on the countertop.

"Are you sure the attorney received it?" Bob asked impatiently.

"Yes, I have a signed receipt. Someone at his law firm received it." Beth Wakefield's lips were drawn into a tight thin line.

Ella's mother retrieved the valuable document after the funeral at Bob's insistence. He'd called her from San Diego while on his trip. He couldn't impress upon her enough how important the document was. Maybe Ella would feel differently now that she knew she'd only get a tiny portion of her father's millions unless she married him. He spent months, weeks, days, trying to convince John Wakefield to put the stipulation into his will. The paperwork was drawn up, but the last time he saw John, he refused to go along with the plan. However, the codicil was expertly forged by Bob's hand. When he returned from San Diego he visited Beth to make sure she had taken it from the vault; she was easily convinced it was John Wakefield's signature. Bob knew he had an ally in Beth Wakefield. She was the only other person who wanted Ella to marry Bob. Making an appeal to her was natural.

Beth was a haughty pretentious woman and when she discovered that Ella left Bob for a common man, an associate attorney without a nickel to his name, she was outraged. His meeting with her today was to forge a strong bond against Ella's relationship with Ray Adriano ~ and, he was succeeding. He had stopped by to discuss the document the day before and Beth bought into the scheme. She insisted on sending it special delivery to the law firm herself.

"I still can't believe Ella walked out on you, Bob." Beth had been fuming since he told her. "And staying in that ugly little beach house in that horrid little neighborhood, I never would have believed Ella could be talked into something like that. But she has been impertinent lately. She has barely spoken with me since her father died, as if his death was my fault or something."

Bob stood in the kitchen as Beth ranted. Good. It was working. The fissure that existed between Ella and her mother was being widened. Beth was on his side in all of this. Maybe she could talk some sense into Ella. Yes. That was the idea.

"Hey, Beth, I've got to get back to the office." Bob mumbled.

"If I hear anything from her, I'll let you know." Beth nodded, but he could tell she was seething. He'd like to be a fly on the wall when Ella arrived to talk with her mother. But, he had no intention of staying. He knew exactly what the conversation would be. *What would their friends think of Ella leaving Bob? Ella would no longer be a member at The Club. How would she, Beth Wakefield, explain this to others in their circle of friends? Why wasn't Ella marrying the man her father had chosen for her? Why was she letting her hormones take over and running off with this Italian from New York City? He was a hoodlum, he had nothing. Ella was an heiress with a family name.*

Bob drove back to his country club house and waited. Seth Bailey was supposed to be calling him soon. He wanted to be alone when he took the call. Seth had a gun with the serial number filed off and he explained to Bob this was the only way to go. But the payment for his services would be much higher, more than he wanted to pay. However, to get rid of Ray Adriano, it would be worth it in the long run.

Ella would be the perfect trophy wife. She was beautiful, intelligent, and once she married him, she'd be one of the richest women in their circle. In fact, her wealth would propel them both into the elite circle that had always been his goal.

Bob glanced at his wrist, damn, his Rolex must be in the master bedroom. Where the hell was Seth? He was fifteen minutes late and if there was anything that aggravated Bob Albertson was tardiness. It smacked of disrespect.

Finally, a knock at the door. But it wasn't Seth Bailey. Detective Sanchez, a plain-clothes detective opened his coat revealing the badge and gun on his belt as he spoke, "Mr. Albertson, I need to speak with you."

Not knowing what to say, Bob invited the man in, but he remained on the stoop.

Sanchez pulled Bob outside and handcuffed him in one fell swoop. "Not here. We're going down to the station to have a nice long chat."

The sick feeling in the pit of his stomach turned from shock to anger. That little bastard must have somehow turned on him. But Seth was the one committing the acts. They could never prove he had anything to do with it.

As Sanchez helped him into the backseat of the blacked-out SUV, Bob Albertson uttered one sentence, "I want my attorney."

She knew dropping in on her mother would infuriate her, but Ella had to get answers. She no longer worried about her mother's delicate feelings. Ray's rental Lexus pulled into the driveway and Ella saw her mother peek around the curtain, she was so obvious. She knew her mother didn't recognize the vehicle. Ella asked Ray to wait a few minutes. Ray smiled and said, "Good luck," but Ella knew luck would have nothing to do with this conversation.

The condo sat on a bluff above the sandy beach of Kennebunk Maine. An exclusive neighborhood, but it was a step down for her mother when the divorce transpired. She was used to living in a private enclave in Falmouth Foreside with a house full of servants tending to her every need. Ella's mother was more concerned with what her society friends thought of her than her own daughter. As Ella rang the doorbell to the million-dollar cottage, the facts were never more evident to her than now.

She imagined her mother was checking the security camera. Ella waited another minute and rang the bell again. After a while, she heard the door unlatch. Ella stared at her mother without as much as a hello. The door opened slightly and Beth Wakefield feigned surprise, "My goodness, Ella, what are you doing here this time of night?"

"I have to talk with you, mother." Ella remained on the stairs.

The door opened wider and Ella walked inside, but she saw her mother glance at the car in the driveway. "Who's that, Ella?'

"My attorney." Ella was now standing in the kitchen. The first thing she noticed was Bob's Rolex sitting on the counter. She turned it over in her hand and saw his initials, "So, you've had a visit from Bob?" Ella asked calmly.

"Yes, he was here. Why do you ask?" Beth Wakefield was a master at skimming the surface, Ella thought.

"I know you sent the codicil along to my attorney's office. And, you realize that it is a forged document, so when I prosecute the person who forged it, you will be an accessory to that crime." Ella stated flatly.

Beth Wakefield's eyes fixed on Ella with disdain. "You wouldn't dare. Those papers were signed by your father. He wanted you to marry Bob!"

"No, mother. You're wrong." Ella contested. "But you are wondering *how* I know you are wrong, aren't you?"

"Yes," Beth Wakefield seemed stunned.

"I met with Marina and she told me that father *refused* to sign those papers, even after Bob pressured him to do it. So, the papers you forwarded were forged. How could you go along with his stupid little conspiracy? Did you know that Bob might even be involved in father's death? It wasn't an accident. There's proof of that."

Ella watched as her mother moved away from her. "You're lying. Bob would never do anything like that ~ why would he?" Ella could see the tiny seed of doubt in her mother's eyes.

"Bob Albertson is not the man you think he is, mother. He dazzled you with his false flattery and all of his money. He worked his charm on father, too. But in the end, it was Marina who saw through him. She convinced father not to go along with his little plan. And, she informed me that father never signed the paperwork." Ella's pulse was racing as she uttered the last words, "I'll see you in court." With that, she slammed the door and walked purposefully to the Lexus waiting for her and Ray drove her away.

Epilogue: Eighteen months later

~ Ella ~

It had been a long year and a half, but she felt it was only right to stop by the Portland Police Department to see Detective Sanchez personally. Ella had never had the opportunity to speak with him alone, to thank him. He was a dedicated professional and if it wasn't for him, there was a good chance that her life could have taken a very different course and her father's killer might have never been discovered.

On the beautiful warm spring day, she pulled into the parking lot and skipped up the stairs into the building that looked more like a modern day museum with no windows. The receptionist buzzed Detective Sanchez and a few moments later he arrived in the lobby to greet her. "Yes, Miss Wakefield, how are you?"

Ella looked into his dark eyes, "I don't know how I can ever thank you enough for all that you've done. The case was airtight. The work you did was exemplary.

"Oh, I just provided the evidence. It was District Attorney Adriano who pushed the case to the top of the pile. He's a pit bull. I've never seen anyone so committed to justice, so passionate for the cause. It's been my pleasure working with him." Sanchez smiled. "Even though he didn't prosecute the case directly, he followed the law to the letter. He's a good man, Miss Wakefield."

Ella couldn't stop herself. She threw her arms around Detective Sanchez and kissed his cheek. "What you did was amazing. I'll never forget you," she whispered in his ear. Not wanting to embarrass him any further, Ella turned and walked toward the door.

"Miss Wakefield," Sanchez called to her. "Yes," Ella turned.

"Say hello to Ray for me." He smiled.

She waved, smiled back, and continued to her vehicle in the parking lot. The Cumberland County District Attorney's office was one block down the street. She drove the one block and parked in the visitor's slot. For a fleeting second, she thought about Bob Albertson in prison with a ten-year sentence. She wondered what sort of view he had from his cell. And, she thought briefly of her mother in a woman's detention facility serving three years. What would her high society friends think of her now? Would they visit her there? Ella doubted it.

As she approached the stately white building, she saw the rugged dark-haired man with sunglasses coming down the stairs toward her. Something stirred inside her when he removed his sunglasses and she gazed into his dark blue eyes. He had a little smirk and a look of defiance about him. His nickname was *The Enforcer*. His hand reached up and tilted Ella's chin just enough so he could kiss her in broad daylight on the steps in front of everyone. But she was proud to be kissing this man who was soon to be her husband in the bustling city square.

"Ready for our vacation at the fishing camp?" he whispered with mischief in his deep blue eyes.

"Yes, I'm ready." Ella whispered. "I've never been so ready. I've fallen for you."

THE END

If you liked this book, please leave a review on Amazon

~ I would personally appreciate it ~

Please check out my other books, romance-thrillers:

The Dark Horse Guardians Series:

A Sense of Duty, Encountering Evil, Flawlessly Executed, and Hard Man to Kill.

Also, The Garden Shed, a children's novella series, perfect for bedtime

The Last Cowboy, Romance

Deep Blue Truth, Romance

Made in the USA
Monee, IL
06 September 2019